THEY'RE OFF!
THE STORY OF
THE PONY EXPRESS

Cheryl Harness

Simon & Schuster Books For Young Readers

SIMON & SCHUSTER BOOKS FOR YOUNG READERS
An imprint of Simon & Schuster Children's Publishing Division
1230 Avenue of the Americas
New York, New York 10020

Book design by Anahid Hamparian
The text of this book is set in 14-point Aldine 721
The illustrations are rendered in watercolor and colored pencil
Printed and bound in the United States of America
First Edition

10 9 8 7 6 5 4 3 2 1

Library of Congress Cataloging-in-Publication Data
Harness, Cheryl.
They're off! : the story of the Pony Express / written
and illustrated by Cheryl Harness.
p.   cm.
Summary: Relates the history of the Pony Express from
when it began to carry messages across
the American West in April 1860 until the telegraph
replaced it in October 1861.
1. Pony express—History—Juvenile literature.
2. Postal service—United States—History—Juvenile literature.
[1. Pony express—History   2. Postal service—History.]   I. Title.
HE6375.P65H37   1996   383'.143'0973—dc20   95-43534   CIP   AC
ISBN: 0-689-80523-3

To the brave young riders
who rode in darkness with
no headlights on their horses.
—C. H.

In the earliest days of the United States, when the young nation had just broken away from England in the Revolutionary War, the West was the mysterious woods beyond the Appalachian Mountains. As the country's population grew, trails were blazed, rivers were navigated, roads were built, canals were dug, and people made their ways to the sunset wilderness.

Before very long, the West began where the eastern railroads, trees, and telegraph wires ended at the muddy Missouri River.

Then adventurers returned home with tales of rich Spanish lands by the far Pacific, two thousand miles away beyond wild plains, mountains, and deserts. Eastern folks began to go see for themselves. When they heard tales of California gold, discovered in 1848, thousands of people rushed into the West as fast as slow wagon trains could go.

Missouri River towns such as St. Joseph and Independence were bursting with people who had arrived by train, stagecoach, and steamboat to outfit their covered wagon caravans. American Indians, tired of strangers trespassing on their lands, and hostile outlaws awaited them on the windy prairies. Cruel deserts and fierce mountain snows made for perilous passage. Still, by 1860, half a million Americans had made it to the new states of Oregon and California. The westerners and the people back east—where talk about war between the North and South was getting mighty hot—were desperate to get letters and newspapers to one another. And the quicker the better!

NEWS TRAVELS SLOWLY...

It was late 1849 before most Americans got word that GOLD had been discovered in California in January of 1848. By 1860, many thousands of homesick gold rushers were desperate for news from the East.

CANADA

NEBRASKA Territory

UTAH · KANSAS Territories

SAN FRANCISCO

3 to 6 weeks

5,200 miles

UNITED STATES

NEW YORK

January 1855 48 miles of jungle railroad completed on the ISTHMUS of PANAMA

CUBA

MEXICO

Central America

PANAMA

OCEAN

VENEZUELA

COLOMBIA

ECUADOR

The EQUATOR

Amazon River

GUYANA SURINAME FRENCH GUIANA

PERU

BOLIVIA

BRAZIL

PACIFIC OCEAN

13,000 miles

"rounding the HORN"

4 months by steamship

PARAGUAY

CHILE

ARGENTINA

URUGUAY

ATLANTIC

CAPE HORN

U·S· MAIL

People and mail often traveled by ocean vessels to avoid the dangers of the land routes. Overland journeys could take from three weeks to six months. But mail by clipper ship or steamboat was unreliable and, at 12 to 80 cents per ounce, very expensive. And, still, TOO SLOW!

Getting the mail from the East to the West and back again was only part of the problem. Clipper ships and steamboats couldn't get the mail to the miners in the mountains or to the settlers in the western towns. The politicians in Washington, D.C., were worried about getting the official U.S. mail over rough country, through all kinds of weather, and past justifiably angry Indians.

The mail had to go, if not by sea, then over land; but which way? The Central Overland Route followed the Oregon and California trails for nearly two thousand miles. Southern congressmen preferred the Southern, or "Ox-Bow," Route. It was eight hundred miles longer, but far from the terrible snowy mountains. And if war should come, the South might win control of the way to rich California. The postmaster general, a southerner, chose this route for the U.S. mail.

In 1858, the Congress voted to give the Butterfield Overland Mail Company three hundred thousand dollars a year to carry the mail east to west and back two times a month.

CANADA

WASHINGTON TERRITORY

Ft. Vancouver

COLUMBIA RIVER

1849
Alexander Todd
began a one-man
mail business.
For 1 ounce of gold ($4)
1 letter was delivered
to a homesick
gold miner.

OREGON TRAIL

SNAKE RIVER

Ft. Hall

NEBRASKA TERRITORY

MISSOURI RIVER

UNORGANIZED TERRITORY

CALIFORNIA TRAIL

1848 GOLD!

Sacramento

San Francisco

Great Salt Lake

Salt Lake City

Ft. Bridger

MORMON TRAIL

Central Overland Route

PLATTE RIVER

1851~1859
George
Chorpenning
and his mules carried
the mail between
SALT LAKE CITY and
SACRAMENTO

UTAH TERRITORY

CHERRY CREEK GOLD 1858

KANSAS TERRITORY

1858~1861 The U.S. GOVERNMENT
gave JOHN BUTTERFIELD money for stagecoaches,
horses, mules, and men to carry the U.S. MAIL
on long, SLOW (50 days there and back) trips
through very HOT deserts in the APACHE and
COMANCHE territories of
NEW MEXICO. DANGEROUS!

NEW MEXICO TERRITORY

SANTA FE

Bent's Fort

SANTA FE TRAIL

mountain division

Cimarron cut-off

TEXAS

INDIAN TERRITORY

RED RIVER

The Butterfield Overland Mail on SOUTHERN or "OX-BOW" Route

This way was chosen by the U.S. MAIL
government for the terrible snowy
to avoid the mountains to the north.

El Paso

RIO GRANDE

San Antonio

PACIFIC

MEXICO

AMERICANS ON THE MOVE...
ON THE BRINK OF **WAR**

LAKE SUPERIOR

MINNESOTA

WISCONSIN

St.Paul

Minneapolis

LAKE HURON

LAKE MICHIGAN

MICHIGAN

Detroit

Milwaukee

IOWA

Davenport

Chicago

ILLINOIS

INDIANA

Nauvoo

LAKE ERIE

Cleveland

OHIO

St.Joseph

St.Louis

Independence

to San Francisco

2812 miles

MISSOURI

ARKANSAS

MISSISSIPPI RIVER

OHIO RIVER

Louisville

KENTUCKY

TENNESSEE

Nashville

LAKE ONTARIO

The ERIE CANAL

1860

5,000 miles of CANALS linked the East

NEW YORK

VERMONT

MAINE

Boston

MASS.

CONN.

R.I.

New York

PENNSYLVANIA

NEW JERSEY

DELAWARE

Philadelphia

MARYLAND

WASHINGTON D.C.

Richmond

VIRGINIA

NORTH CAROLINA

Raleigh

ATLANTIC

1830

"The Best Friend of CHARLESTON" was the 1st steam locomotive in regular service. 30,000 miles of railroad crisscrossed the East by 1860. Trains went nearly 60 miles per hour!

SOUTH CAROLINA

Charleston

Atlanta

GEORGIA

Savannah

NATCHEZ

Vicksburg

LOUISIANA

MISSISSIPPI

ALABAMA

New Orleans

FLORIDA

free states

slave states

territories

Would the practice of SLAVERY extend into the U.S. territories? That was the question.

For three years, until the southern states left the Union and the Civil War erupted, bright red or green Butterfield stagecoaches carried the U.S. mail between Tipton, Missouri, and San Francisco. Three weeks each way they went through boiling sun, rain, snow, and the whizzing bullets and arrows of Apache and Comanche warriors.

All this time, many northerners and westerners campaigned for the Central Route. It would bring the mail closer to the new gold mines in Colorado. But still the Congress was reluctant: too many people had frozen to death in mountain snowstorms. It would take a new, dramatic idea, one that would catch the public's imagination. Fast. Exciting. Death-defying.

It was getting to be time for the ponies.

It wasn't an absolutely new idea.
People had ridden horses in relays to carry the news across the Persian

Empire, the Roman Empire, and across the kingdom of the Great Khan of medieval China. Why not across the American West? wondered two men riding horseback along the Central Route in the fall of 1854.

One of the men was California senator Gwin, on his way to Washington, D.C. The other was B. F. Ficklin, superintendent of the great freight-hauling, wagon train, and stagecoach company, Russell, Majors, and Waddell.

Wasn't it only last winter that relay riders from the Adams and Wells Fargo Express Companies had carried a presidential message from San Francisco up to Portland? The two men agreed that lightning-fast couriers between Missouri and California would be just the ticket—that is, if they could get anyone else to go along with the idea.

The forces of business and politics sometimes move as slowly as an ox-drawn wagon. Then *BANG,* as fast as a pony shooting out of a St. Joe stable, an idea becomes a reality because the time is right.

That time was January 27, 1860. B. F. Ficklin's boss, William H. Russell, sent a telegram to his son: "Have determined to establish a Pony Express to Sacramento, California, commencing 3rd of April. Time ten days."

The colorful names of the PONY EXPRESS stations often came from wilderness landmarks.

I made myself a prosperous man of business in Lexington, Missouri.

I was known as a stern religious man who knew well how to work with men, mules, and oxen.

We got together in 1855 to sell goods, wagons, and stock to travelers and to haul freight across the western frontier.

WILLIAM H. RUSSELL

ALEXANDER MAJORS

WILLIAM BRADFORD WADDELL
a descendant of PILGRIM Gov. William BRADFORD

This optimistic frontier businessman, who saw an opportunity to compete with Mr. Butterfield's stagecoaches and get the government mail contract, had to do a lot of convincing to get his cautious partners to go along. Alexander Majors and William Bradford Waddell reluctantly agreed to back Russell in the expensive proposition.

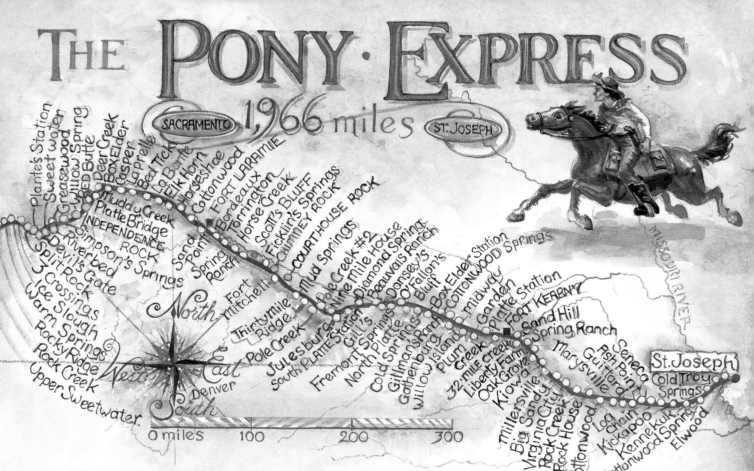

THE PONY · EXPRESS

SACRAMENTO 1,966 miles **St. Joseph**

They called their new company the Central Overland California and Pikes Peak Express Company. In only sixty-five days the race would begin. But first, five hundred of the very best horses must be bought. First-class thoroughbreds and California mustangs were strong and fast enough to run the ten to fifteen miles between relay stations in about an hour. Pony Express stations were built of adobe, logs, or sod in between the forts and stagecoach stations; there were nearly 190 stops in all.

People had to be hired to tend the horses and mind the stations. Hay and feed had to be bought to feed the horses; bacon, flour, and coffee to feed the people. Posters and newspaper advertisements said:

YOUNG SKINNY WIRY FELLOWS

NOT OVER EIGHTEEN. MUST BE EXPERT

RIDERS WILLING TO RISK DEATH DAILY.

ORPHANS PREFERRED.

WAGES $25 PER WEEK.

Eighty young men were hired to ride for the Pony Express. All in all, the new company had spent one hundred thousand dollars. Everything was set to go for the day the nation had been waiting for. Tomorrow the ponies would ride!

THEY'RE OFF!
TUESDAY, APRIL 3, 1860

SAN FRANCISCO, CALIFORNIA—4:00 P.M.

The crowd in front of the Alta Telegraph Company cheered
as the mochila was thrown over the saddle of the buff-colored pony.
A woman tied her bonnet on the pony's head. "For luck!" she called as
James Randall rode away to the waterfront and onto the deck of the
Antelope. This steamboat would carry them to Sacramento, California,
where the long race would really begin, late in the rainy night.

ST. JOSEPH, MISSOURI—5:00 P.M.

The mail train from Hannibal was late! As a brass band played, excited folks pulled hairs from the tail of a nervous little bay mare—for souvenirs. Her rider led her back to the stable. Finally the steam whistle! The speeches! The cannon! It was 7:15 by the time Johnny Fry pounded away to the ferry landing and across the Missouri River. Gotta make up time!

The MOCHILA (mo·CHEE·la) is designed to go over the SADDLE~and off again~ in a hurry. It has four mail pouches called CANTINAS.

SALT LAKE CITY

Sacramento

ANTELOPE

San Francisco

After riding 6 to 8 different horses as fast as they could go, the rider came to a "home station" where he rested awhile before heading 75 to 100 miles back the way he came to the home station at the other end of his route. He ate beans and bacon with the station keepers, stock tenders, and stagecoach drivers. Wagon trains brought provisions to the PONY EXPRESS stations. Horse thieves and hostile Indians brought danger.

Billy Hamilton would take the mail at Sacramento. While he waited for the steamboat from San Francisco, Johnny Fry's horse was galloping through the spring night in eastern Kansas, nearly two thousand miles away. He rode almost seventy miles to Kickapoo Station, where Don Rising was impatiently waiting to ride on to Marysville. Don passed the mail on to Jack Keetley.

"There he goes!" yelled the travelers in the creaking slow wagon trains. With a wave, Jack was gone down the trail, and he vanished at the flat horizon.

After Fort Kearny stretched miles of buffalo country. The great, shaggy animals followed the racing pony and the red-shirted rider with their eyes. Past stagecoaches and Indian camps, the surefooted ponies made their way over Rocky Mountain trails.

Once the PONY EXPRESS was in full operation, 80 or more determined riders between the ages of 11 and 45 were out riding night and day.

FORT LARAMIE

CHIMNEY ROCK

JULESBURG

FORT KEARNY

Old Patee House

PONY EXPRESS OFFICES

St. Joseph

Six days out of St. Joe, a lone rider pounded through a cloud of dust into Salt Lake City. Four stormy days later, after seven hundred miles of hard desert and mountain relay-riding, Billy Hamilton and the westbound mail were greeted by the people of Sacramento at 5:25 P.M. on the evening of April 13.

Ten days earlier, Billy Hamilton had thundered out of Sacramento, eastward into a black rainy night. He rode five different horses fifty-seven miles till the morning of April 4, then Warren Upson flung the mochila over his mustang's saddle. The worst part of the trail of the Pony Express lay before him: the steep, dangerous Sierra Nevada, thick with snow, wild with icy wind, deep with canyons.

After finishing their ten- to fifteen-mile runs, the cold, trembling horses rested in the stalls of the mountain stations as the young rider, on a fresh mount, continued on. Eighty-five miles later, Warren passed the eastbound mail on to "Pony Bob" Haslam; then Howard Egan and others raced on. Somewhere east of Salt Lake City, sometime on Sunday, April 8, a young man headed west passed another going east.

Horse by horse, rider by rider, the scuffed, scarred mochila sped on day and night. It was nearly lost in the rain-swollen Platte River when a horse was swept away in the current and downstream into quicksand! The rider scrambled off with the mail and onto a horse belonging to one of the folks watching from the riverbank. With a cheer they waved him on, then rescued the poor horse.

Henry Wallace, Jack Keetley, Don Rising, and finally Johnny Fry hurried from Marysville on the last relay to St. Joe. Johnny made it by five in the evening of April 13, ten days since he'd left there with the mail from the East.

Billy Hamilton had ridden off alone in a rainy night; now the whooping, bell clanging, cannon fire, and hip-hurrahs astonished him and his tired pony on the evening of April 13 in Sacramento. As fast as the mail was sorted, the cantinas were locked, and the mochila was thrown back on the pony's saddle, Billy raced to the *Antelope*, which was waiting to sail to San Francisco.

Midnight parades! Bonfires and rockets! Californians were connected with their fellow citizens—and in less than half the time that the Butterfield stage had taken. Ten days! Hurrah!

PONY EXPRESS

Earlier on that legendary night of April 13, 1860, Johnny Fry and his horse rested on the Missouri River ferry from Elwood, Kansas, over to St. Joseph, Missouri. Cheering crowds surrounded them as Johnny dismounted in front of the Pony Express offices in the Patee House hotel. The spring night was full of church bells, fireworks, and gunsmoke. The Great Breakthrough Adventure was a success—for now.

HURRAH for the PONY!!

The Pony Express began at a time when the country was about to go to war with itself: the Civil War between the northern and southern states. And another war was going on between old and new Americans as treaties were broken, buffalo were killed, and Indians were run out of their lands.

Angry, hungry Paiutes went to war in the deserts and canyons of the Utah Territory in May 1860. One Pony Express rider was so scared of Paiutes on the warpath that he refused to ride. That's when Pony Bob Haslam became a legend, riding 380 miles in thirty-six hours with only a few hours' rest.

For three weeks the Pony Express was shut down. Even after the Indians quieted, with the help of Paiute chief Young Winnemucca and others, there were still raids and attacks along the trail of the Pony Express. Horses were stolen, stations were burned to the ground, and sixteen men, including an Express rider, were killed. His horse carried the mail to the next relay station all by himself. Another rider, fifteen-year-old Nick Wilson, was shot in the forehead with an arrow. He survived, and until his death at the age of seventy-one, Nick wore his hat pulled low to hide the scar.

Seventy-five thousand dollars. That's what it cost to get the ponies going after the Paiute War. Mr. Russell kept hoping that the government would help pay for the Pony Express, but the contract for the U.S. mail still went to the Butterfield stagecoaches on the Ox-Bow Route in the South. Mr. Russell and his gloomy partners increased service to twice a week and went deeper in debt. It cost their company thirty-eight dollars in wages and horse feed to deliver a letter that a customer had paid two to ten dollars to send.

Back and forth across the West went the ponies. In November 1860, the westbound mochila carried the results of the presidential election. Eastern newspapers, specially printed on lightweight paper and wrapped in oiled silk to protect them from snow and icy rivers, were locked up in the cantinas. Soon the news traveled through the western states, crackling along the telegraph wires between Fort Churchill and San Francisco: Abe Lincoln was president!

THE UNION MUST AND SHALL BE PRESERVED

FREE SPEECH
FREE HOMES
FREE TERRITORY

PROTECTION TO AMERICAN INDUSTRY

For President
ABRAHAM LINCOLN
OF ILLINOIS

For Vice President
HANNIBAL HAMLIN
OF MAINE

In spite of the bosses' money problems, the tough riders and ponies valiantly carried the mail back and forth across the frontier. Around campfires, in fancy parlors, and in settlers' cabins, amazing tales were told about the riders' cool courage, quick thinking, devotion to duty, and narrow escapes from danger.

One dark night, twenty-year-old Howard Egan was riding through a canyon when he and his pony saw firelight flickering off in the blackness. Indians!

Howard made a quick decision. Striking his spurs into the pony, he yelled *"Eeeeeowoooeeiee!"* and charged straight through the Indian camp. Hoofbeats and gunshots from Howard's Colt revolver echoed off the walls of the canyons. He escaped! Later he found out that the Indians were waiting to catch one of the Express riders to see what they were carrying in such a hurry.

"Buffalo Bill" Cody earned his name killing buffalo. Kings and queens and everybody came to see his "Wild West Show." Bill loved to tell about when he was a fifteen-year-old Pony Express rider who had once ridden 384 miles with no rest. Another rider, George Little, was barely sixteen when his horse gave out in a fierce snowstorm. George cut the cantinas on the mochila, stuffed the mail in his shirt, and fought his way through the snow on foot to Salt Lake City.

March 4, 1861. The whole nation wanted to know what Mr. Lincoln would say after he took his oath of office. Could his words stop the southern states from leaving the Union? Would there be war? Seven days and seventeen hours—and the lives of two horses—was what it took to get the president's speech to the West. The fastest time ever: the young riders and ponies sped over hundreds of miles of danger.

The South *did* leave the Union in spite of the president's peacemaking words: "We must not be enemies." The Civil War exploded in April and the ponies carried the news. All the while Russell, Majors, and Waddell's business was ruined, deep in debt. What ended the Pony Express, though—and it was ending—was a new race across the western lands.

Work gangs of men were racing to dig holes for almost forty thousand wooden poles and then to connect the wooden poles with wire. Telegraph wire. One crew worked east, the other west. When the wires met in the middle, messages could be sent by electricity—faster by far than the fastest pony. How could a pony compete with lightning?

The eastern and western states were connected with the "talking wires" pole to pole in Salt Lake City on October 24, 1861. Just two days later, the Pony Express was ended.

The United States of America started up along the eastern edge of the continent and ended up spreading clear out to the Pacific Ocean. Thousands and thousands of all kinds of people, horses, mules, and oxen lived hard and died to make this happen. A whole Indian way of life was shoved out of the way to make this happen.

The ponies had run more than 600,000 miles with 34,753 pieces of mail. By helping Americans write to one another, the Pony Express helped to keep the East and West together at a time when the nation, North and South, was pulling apart. The brave young riders and their ponies helped to make a nation happen.

Not by a long shot was it the last adventure in beating the western wilderness: seven and a half years of railroad tracks racing to meet at the Golden Spike were just ahead. But it's the ponies and the daring young men who ride in our imagination.

When the wind is in the West, listen for distant hoofbeats.

It's the Pony Express.

PONY EXPRESS RIDERS

1. John Anson
2. Henry Avis
3. Rodney Babbit
4. Lafayette Ball
5. James Banks
6. James Barnell
7. Melville Baughn
8. Jim Baugn
9. Marve Beardsley
10. James Beatley
11. Charles Becker
12. Tom Bedford
13. Charles Billman
14. G. R. Bills
15. Black Sam
16. Black Tom
17. Lafayette "Bolly" Bolwinkle Bond
18. Jim "Boston"
19. William Boulton
20. John Brandenburger
21. James Brink
22. Hugh Brown
23. James Brown
24. James (Jimmy) Bucklin
25. John Burnett
26. Ed Bush
27. William Campbell
28. Alexander Carlyle
29. William (Bill) Carr
30. William Carrigan
31. William A. (Bill) Cates
32. James (Jimmy) Clark
33. John Clark
34. Richard Cleve
35. Charley Cliff
36. Gustavas (Gus) Cliff
37. William F. (Bill) Cody
38. Buck Cole
39. Bill Corbett
40. Edward Covington
41. Jack Crawford
42. James Cumbo
43. James Danley
44. Louis Dean
45. William (Bill) Dennis
46. Frank Derrick
47. Alex Diffenbacher
48. Thomas Dobson
49. J. Dodge
50. Joseph (Joe) Donovan
51. Tom Donvan
52. W. E. Dorrington
53. Calvin Downs
54. Daniel M. Drumheller
55. James E. Dunlap
56. William Eckels
57. Howard R. Egan
58. Major Howard Egan
59. Richard E. (Ras) Egan
60. Tom J. Elliot
61. J. K. Ellis
62. Charles Enos
63. George Fair
64. H. J. Faust
65. Johnny Fischer
66. John Fisher
67. William (Billy) Fisher
68. Thomas Flynn
69. Jimmie Foreman
70. Johnny Fry
71. Abram Fuller
72. George Gardner
73. James (Jim) Gentry
74. James Gilson
75. Samuel Gilson
76. Frank Gould
77. "Irish Tom" Grady
78. Sam Hall
79. Billy Hamilton
80. Samuel (Sam) Hamilton
81. Robert "Pony Bob" Haslam
82. Theodore Hawkins
83. Sam Haws
84. Frank Helvey
85. Levi Hensel
86. Charles Higginbotham
87. Clark Hogan
88. Martin Hogan
89. Lester (Let) Huntington
90. "Irish Jim"
91. William (Bill) James
92. David R. Jay
93. William D. Jenkins
94. Samuel S. Jobe
95. William Jones
96. J. H. (Jack) Keetley
97. Jay G. Kelley
98. Mike Kelly
99. Thomas O. King
100. John Phillip Koerner
101. Harry LaMont
102. Bob Lancaster
103. George E. Little
104. "Little Yank"
105. "Tough" Littleton
106. N. N. Lytle
107. Sye Macaulus
108. Robert Martin
109. Elijah Maxfield
110. Montgomery Maze
111. J. G. McCall
112. James (Jim) McDonald
113. Pat McEneany
114. David McLaughlin
115. James McNaughton
116. William McNaughton
117. Lorenzo Meacona
118. J. P. Mellen
119. Howard Mifflin
120. "Broncho" Charley Miller✛
121. James Moore
122. John T. Moss
123. Jeramiah H. Murphy
124. Newton Myrick
125. and 126. Matt and Robert Orr
127. G. Packard
128. William Page
129. Zachary Taylor Parshall
130. "Mochila Joe" Paxton
131. G. W. (Josh) Perkins
132. William Pridham
133. Thomas Ranahan
134. James Randall
135. Theodore "Yank" Rank
136. Charles Reynolds
137. Thomas J. Reynolds
138. William Minor Richards
139. Johnson William Richardson
140. Jonathan Rinehart
141. Bart Riles
142. Don Rising
143. Harry Roff
144. Edward Rush
145. Robert Sanders
146. G. G. Sangiovanni
147. George Scovell
148. John Seerbeck
149. Jack Selman
150. Joe Serish
151. John Sinclair
152. Jack Slade
153. George Spurr
154. William H. Streeper
155. Robert C. Strickland
156. William Strohm
157. John Sugget
158. Billy Tate
159. Josiah Taylor
160. George Thatcher
161. J. J. Thomas
162. Charles P. Thompson
163. Charlie "Cyclone" Thompson
164. James M. Thompson
165. Alexander Topence
166. W. S. Tough
167. George Towne
168. Henry Tuckett
169. Warren Upson
170. William E. Van Blaricon
171. John Garner Vincent
172. John B. Wade
173. Henry Wallace
174. Daniel Westcott
175. Michael M. Whalen
176. "Whipsaw"
177. H. C. Wills
178. Elijah Nicholas Wilson
179. Joseph B. Wintle
180. Henry Worley
181. James Worthington
182. Jose Zowgalatz

✛ last surviving Pony Express rider, died January 15, 1955, in New York City at the age of 105

THANKS TO THE STAFF OF THE ST. JOSEPH MUSEUM AND THE PONY EXPRESS MUSEUM

Around the World in the Days of the PONY EXPRESS
April 3, 1860 — October 26, 1861

Mediterranean Sea · Port Said · NILE · EGYPT · Cairo · Suez · SINAI Peninsula · RED SEA

Construction is underway on the SUEZ CANAL so you can go from EUROPE to ASIA without having to go all the way around AFRICA.

QUEEN VICTORIA reigns over the EMPIRE of GREAT BRITAIN 1837~1901

~1850~1864~ millions of Chinese die in TAIPING Rebellion

·JULY 21, 1861· First BATTLE of BULL RUN (MANASSAS) 3,500 men dead & wounded

Abraham LINCOLN is elected November 6, 1860

SOUTH CAROLINA secedes from ~leaves~ the UNION December 20, 1860 the Confederate government is formed February 4, 1861

CZAR ALEXANDER II frees the SERFS, Russian peasants bound to work the land owned by the aristocrats.

Giuseppe GARIBALDI led 1,000 men, "RED SHIRTS," in battle to unite ITALY

fashionable European and American girls wore "GARIBALDI" shirts with their hoop skirts, crinolines and petticoats.

Etienne Lenoir invented a practical internal combustion engine

BIBLIOGRAPHY

Billington, Ray Allen, and Martin Ridge. *Westward Expansion: A History of the American Frontier.* New York: Macmillan, 1982.

Dicerto, Joseph J. *The Pony Express: Hoofbeats in the Wilderness.* New York: Franklin Watts, 1989.

Hafen, Le Roy R. *The Overland Mail.* New York: AMS Press, 1969.

Reinfeld, Fred. *Pony Express.* New York: Macmillan, 1966.

Settle, Raymond W., and Mary Lund Settle. *Saddles and Spurs: The Pony Express Saga.* Lincoln: University of Nebraska Press, 1972.

Smith, Waddell F. *The Story of the Pony Express.* San Rafael, Calif.: Pony Express History and Art Gallery, 1964.

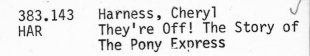